Contents

Chapter 1   The Beginning

Chapter 2   My New Friend

Chapter 3   Lights

Chapter 4   The Family   21

Chapter 5   School   27

Chapter 6   Peter's Hide Out   33

Chapter 7   Special Powers   39

Chapter 8   Preparations   47

Chapter 9   The Big Day   55

Chapter 10   The Game   63

Chapter 11   The End   72

Chapter 12   Help   81

Chapter 13   Holidays   84

Chapter 1

The Beginning

I landed with a bang; my head hurt and felt very hot, where was I? I had been travelling through the air for what seemed like a lifetime.

I pressed the release button, and the door of my spaceship opened. It was dark, I couldn't see anything, I could only hear a familiar sound, a sound that I had heard before. It was a light rustle of leaves, made by the wind; it was like Mother Nature was whispering a secret.

Very slowly I stood up. My head was thumping from the inside. Carefully I climbed out of my ship, the ground beneath me was rough and uneven. Where was I?

What was that? I listened again, concentrating this time to see if I could recognise the noise, to see if I could work out what it was. It was screeching and squawking as if a dog and bird were fighting.

I climbed back into my ship and closed the door tight. I was scared and wanted to spend the night where I knew it was safe.

Still listening to the different sounds around me, I tried to work out where I could be. Soon my eyes grew tired, I fell asleep and started to dream.

"Jonny it's time", said my chief.

I had just had my 12th birthday at home on planet Mars, and was preparing, getting ready, to go on my first drive in space alone.

During the flight things went horribly wrong, my ship took control, heading in the opposite direction away from home. Then I landed with a bang.

I woke **suddenly,** and **quickly** sat up, my ship was **shak**ing and something was beating it. I looked out of the window and couldn't **believe** what I saw; a deer was hitting its antlers **against** the ship.

"GET OUT OF MY WAY! GET OUT OF MY WAY! A WOLF IS COMING, GET OUT OF MY WAY, I NEED TO PASS." The deer **scream**ed.

(Thankfully at home we are given the gift to talk and understand animals; they live as **equals amongst** us. They could do the same as us, and go wherever we could go).

Even at home, wolves are bad and are **prepare**d to kill anything that gets in their way. I knew we were both in danger, and I had to help.

Saying nothing, I quickly opened up the ship and jumped out, **ignor**ing the sharp ground cutting my feet. I tried to focus, looking around for something to protect us. I could hear the barking yips and the beating of paws **against** the path. I could hear for miles, so I knew I had a little time, but the wolf was coming and coming fast.

"Quick, try and find something sharp I can use to **defend** us!" I shouted.

The deer froze and just looked at me **confus**ed, as if he couldn't work out why he could understand me. I **remember**ed my chief told me, not every planet talks to or **communicate**s with other animals.

"I shall explain later, just help," I ordered.

Then I heard it; a deep panting sound, it was **growl**ing softly, the sound was like death **itsel**f. I looked up to find the wolf **star**ing at me **sn**arling, **s**aliva dripping from his mouth.

He reared up on his back legs with his mouth open showing me his very sharp and extra dirty teeth. As his claws came down towards me I rolled away, but he was coming at me again, quick as lightening.

I rolled in the opposite direction and felt something sharp stick into my leg; it had torn through my jeans and dug into my skin. At first I couldn't move, I turned my head to see the wolf running towards me howling with joy. I closed my eyes and knew this was the end. I waited for it to attack.

Nothing happened; instead I heard a loud howl, my eyes opened to see the wolf flying above my head. The deer had run into him with his antlers and thrown him through the air. The wolf didn't land too far away, and before I knew it he was on his feet again.

He was back ready to dig his teeth in me. I found just enough strength to pull out the sharp stick from my leg, and push it deep into the wolf's neck.

Chapter Two

My New Friend

We just sat still and quiet for a while. I had never killed anything before, not even an insect. My whole body started to shake, and I felt very cold. My leg hurt from where the stick had dug in, and it was **bleed**ing.

The deer came and **c**url**e**d itself around me to keep me warm. After a while he asked,

'Why can you understand me?'

I **explaine**d where I came from, and what had **happen**e**d** to me.

I needed to fix my leg. Slowly I **crawl**ed back to the ship. Inside I had some sap, which I rubbed on the **w**ound. (Sap is a watery **liqu**id that can be found in plants. We use it at home to heal **injur**ies, to make them better).

'What's your name?' I asked the deer.

'Devin,' he replied.

'Hi Devin, I'm Jonny, why were you here by yourself in the dark, do you not have a family?'

Devin **explaine**d how he was **separate**d from his friends when the wolf came to attack. The herd ran off, but Devin was **scared** and ran in the **opposite** direction, the wolf followed him.

We were alone, lost and **hu**n**g**ry. I didn't know how to get home or whether I would ever see my family again. My ship was badly **dam**aged after the crash and I couldn't fly it.

Dawn was **breaking**, and the sun started to rise. I could start to see what was around me; there were tall trees in every **direction** going on for miles. A fine mist **weaved** its way **through** the **branches** and I could start to hear the **different** sounds of birds singing and **creatures** waking.

Feeling a little braver Devin went off to find some food, this gave me time to think of a plan. Where was I? I knew I was on another planet but which one? Everything was so **similar** to home but I **sensed** even though it felt the same, it was also very **different**. I needed to find **shelter**, somewhere safe and I needed to find out whether there were other people like me living here.

Out of the corner of my eye I noticed the wolf's dead body lying near where I was sitting. I knew the rest of his pack would be coming to look for him soon, so with all the **energy** I could find I **dragged** his body away from the ship to some overgrown fern, and covered him up.

Devin came back a while later with lots of red and black berries wrapped up in a huge green leaf. I sat down rested my back on the ship and began to eat.

While we were filling our **stomachs** with berries, Devin **explained** to me that I was on planet Earth. Here people (who looked like me) rule it. They live **amongst** themselves, some were good and others not. He didn't know much more about them, I would have to find that out myself.

I **decided** that I needed to find where these people lived maybe they could help me. Devin had seen lights before and thought he knew the way.

I packed a bag with things that I would need, hid my ship as best I could by putting leaves and **branches** around the bottom of it. I switched on the **invisibility shield** and watched it disappear (I needed the leaves to be able to find it again). I set off on my first **adventure**.

We walked all day only stopping for a short time to rest my leg, as the sun began to set we found **shel**ter under some large rocks and I **curl**ed up next to Devin for warmth and **tried** to get some sleep.

The next day I walked until my feet could move no **furthe**r, I was dirty and my jeans were ripped. I was tired, cold, **hungr**y and weak.

Then everything went black.

Chapter 3

Lights

At first my eyes would not open, as hard as I **tried** they stayed shut. Although, I could hear, there was a lot of **noise** like alarms or **sirens** and people shouting.

Then I felt someone lift me up and put me in something that moved. I seemed to be **travel**ling fast with the **sir**en still going, but the shouting had stopped.

I tried to work out what was **happening**. Where was Devin? I was too **tire**d to think and everything went still again.

When I woke up, I was alone in a special room. I **tried** to sit up, but I felt so weak and I had a needle sticking into the vein in my hand, it was **attach**ed to a short **plastic** tube. I looked around to see if I could work out where I was when I saw a women walk into the room. She came up to me and put some **fluid**, a clear **liqu**id, in the tube.

"Hello" she said in a soft, **gentle** voice, "my name is Nurse Ann. You were found in the woods. Do you know where you are now?"

I looked around again the room was white and very clean. It only had a chair, bed and a few **ma**chines next to me **bee**ping. I shook my head at Nurse Ann.

"No" I **re**plied, "my name is Jonny. I landed in the woods, I don't know where I am?"

Her face looked **confused**, maybe it was because I had just told her that I had landed in the woods. I wasn't sure but I had the feeling that I should not mention that my home is planet Mars, and my only friend on planet Earth is a deer called Devin. Which **re**minded me, where was Devin?

"Was I alone in the woods?" I asked.

"Yes dear" Nurse Ann **re**plied, "but you were covered in leaves as if someone was trying to keep you warm."

That must have been Devin, I must find him and see if he is ok.

"Great" I said, " I feel much better now, thank you for looking after me. If I can just have my backpack I will leave"

A **shocked** Nurse Ann **re**plied,

"Oh no Jonny, you can't leave without your family or an adult to pick you up. Do you have a contact number of the people who look after you? Do you have any family?"

I laid back down not saying a word; I was **trapped** in this place until my family could pick me up. My family was back on Mars, and had no idea where I was.

"You looked **tired** Jonny" Nurse Ann **continued**, "We are not sure how long you were asleep for, you must rest, I shall go and get you something to eat."

I saw a TV in the corner of the room, I knew what it was as we have them at home. I put it on and **tried** to understand more about these people and how they live. TV show after TV show, showed families living together, adults looking after their children. They were eating, playing and going out together. I missed my family so much. What was going to happen to me? I didn't want an adult to look after me and tell me what to do here on Earth.

A little while later, a tall thin man and a shorter woman, both dressed in smart clothes walked into my room.

"Hello Jonny" the man said, "my name is Doctor Flan and this is Miss Smith. We are here to see how you are feeling and how we can get you back to your family."

Back home I **th**ought, feeling **ex**cited that I might see my parents, brother and sister again. How do they know where my home is, maybe they found my ship in the woods.

"Can you tell me why you were in the woods alone Jonny," he **continu**ed, "Do you have a telephone number of your parents or whoever looks after you. Maybe we could call them, they must be worried."

My heart sank, I felt so sad, he didn't know I was from Mars and he didn't know how to get me home to my family. Tears started to fill my eyes.

Chapter 4

The Family

I didn't say much to anyone after Dr Flan and Miss Smith's visit. I couldn't see the point of talking and I didn't know what to say anyway, I knew no one would **believe** me.

After what seemed like years (but was more like three weeks), the adults **decided** that I should leave the hospital and stay with a family outside of the city. I was to stay there until the police could contact my own family to come and collect me. Being as my family lived in Mars I couldn't see that **happening**.

Miss Smith drove me through the city; it was busy with tall **buildings**, lights, cars and people everywhere. A little while later, we came out of the city and started to drive down a **narrow** road **surrounded** by hills and trees. I could see the woods in the **distance**. I didn't know where I was going, I felt **scared** and **nervous**.

We drove down a steep hill into a **village**. In the middle of the **village** was a car park, which was **surrounded** by houses where **different families** lived.

Miss Smith got out of the car first and then helped me climb out. I picked up my backpack and started to follow her to one of the houses.

Miss Smith **knocked** on the door and a lady **answered**. She had long dark hair, and a **friendly** face with warm **hazelnut** coloured eyes.

"Hello Sarah" Miss Smith said, "this is Jonny, the boy I told you about."

Sarah gave me a big smile and put her hand out for me to shake.

"Hello Jonny and welcome, my name is Sarah. Why don't you come in and I shall go and make us a drink."

I smiled and **quiet**ly said hello back. As we walked through the house I **noticed** other toys, skateboards, computer games and teddy bears lying around. Other children must live here too.

Sarah spotted me looking and told me that she also looked after some other children, two girls and a boy. They were at school and would be soon back. (School? I didn't know what a school was and wondered if it was like the space camp I went to back at home.) Sarah asked if I wanted to have a look at the toys while she finished speaking to Miss Smith. I sat down, smiled and tried to work things out.

There were books on the table with pictures of **different** spaceships; I picked it up to see if I could find one like mine.

It didn't seem long before Miss Smith and Sarah came back into the room. Miss Smith **thank**ed Sarah, said goodbye to me and left. I felt so lost and alone. I wished I could speak to Devin, but I didn't even know where he was anymore.

A little while later the other kids came back home. Amy was the oldest girl; she was 16 years old, and very cool. She had pale skin, long golden hair and dark brown eyes. She also had a warm smile. I liked her **straigh**t the way.

Then there was Tom he was 15 years old, he was covered in mud and holding a ball. He was tall, thin with short curly hair and he had the same dark eyes as Amy. He came up to me gave me a hard slap on the back and a big **tooth**y smile, said hello and walked into the kitchen to look for a snack.

Standing in the doorway was Beth, she didn't smile at all; she just stood still, **star**ing at me. She was only one year younger than me and she had bright green eyes that almost **tw**inkled. I felt like I had met her already, but that was **im**possible, I have never been to this planet before.

"Never mind her," Amy said **cheerful**ly, "she isn't always this weird, I don't know what's got into her today. Come on, let me show you to your room, you are **sharing** with Tom".

Chapter 5

School

It was my first day at school, I felt **nerv**ous but Tom told me not to worry, it would be ok, and he would always be around if I needed him.

The family looking after me were great, they made me feel safe but also they **treat**ed me a little **different**, as if they knew something that I didn't. Maybe they did know that I was from Mars, they never said anything but they never left me alone. It was like they were **protecting** me. Beth hardly spoke, when she did it was always a one-word answer to my questions. I **wonder**ed what I had done to upset her.

Tom was wrong about my first day of school, it was anything but ok.

I walked into the classroom, where my teacher **introduce**d me to my classmates. Everyone seemed **friend**ly apart from two boys at the back of the class. They looked **ident**ical, **ex**actly the same with short, black, spiky hair. They were tall and looked very strong. From a distance their eyes were a dark blue, but when I looked closely there was a hint of **pur**ple. I had seen those eyes before, but I didn't know where from.

"Jonny", my teacher said taking me over to the boys, "meet Sam and Darren, they are brothers who only joined the school last week."

I said hello to the boys but they just **growl**ed in return with a look of hate in their eyes. My teacher spoke to them.

"Now you know what to do in school boys, I would like you to help Jonny **settle** in and keep an eye on him".

Darren **replied**, " Oh don't worry Miss, we will keep a very good eye on him", then they both looked at each other and **sn**ickered, a broken **lau**gh, as if they had a plan that was not good.

The rest of the morning I sat at my desk next to a nice boy called Peter, he was small, wore glasses and wouldn't stop talking. I couldn't **concentrate** or focus on what the teacher was saying, because I was trying to work out where I had seen those boy's eyes before. They were so **familiar** like I knew them, I just couldn't **re**mem**ber** where, but I knew they were bad news.

Why did I **recogni**se Beth and these boys when I had never been on Earth before?

The bell rang and we all went for lunch. I sat with Peter and ate the sandwiches Sarah had packed for me. Sam and Darren came and sat down **opp**os**i**te me on the other side of the table and started **w**hi**spering quiet**ly to each other.

With my super hearing I could hear what they were saying, Darren spoke first.

"Is that him; the one who was sent to Earth?"

Sam **replied**, "Everything looks right, he looks like he is from Mars. What shall we do, we need to be sure?"

Darren said "Lets just watch him for a few days. It is **important** that we get it right, otherwise the Chief will be angry."

Jack nodded his head and **answer**ed 'Ok your right, lets wait for the game on Friday. That's our deadline, we need to **inva**de the school and wipe out the kids **memories** before the weekend".

All of a **sudd**en I felt sick and faint, the blood **drain**ed from my face and my head felt dizzy. I couldn't think **clear**ly. When I crashed and landed on Earth I thought it was an **accid**ent but I was wrong. It was all planned, I am here to save the children, I have never had to save anyone before apart from Devin. I had to save him from the wolf. I **wonder**ed if Devin was still safe, I thought about where he was right now. I wished I could see him.

Peter gave me a **worried** look:

"What is wrong Jonny?" he asked, "You look like your going to be sick".

"I think I might be Peter, " I **re**plied, "I need to find a **quiet** place to think, somewhere were Sam and Darren can't find me."

Peter got **excited,** "I know just the place Jonny" he said, "**qu**ickly follow me".

Chapter 6

Peters Hide Out

Peter led me passed the football pitch to the back of the school, which faced the woods (I **won**dered if Devin was in there somewhere). At the back of a school was a small, old and rundown hut, with its door locked.

"This way," Peter said **excited**ly, "everyone thinks this door is always locked even the Janitor, but I have the key. I have been coming here for five years now with no-one **k**nowing. Come on I shall show you inside."

Peter opened the door and I couldn't **belie**ve what I saw, nothing, there was **noth**ing there, just an **em**pty room. I **th**ought maybe Peter was a little crazy, so I just looked, nodded and told him it was cool.

"Don't be silly Jonny," Peter said as if I were crazy too, "this is just the **en**tran**c**e, follow me and I'll take you inside".

I followed Peter into the small hut, and watched while he felt around the walls, and then he turned to me looking a bit **em**barrass**e**d:

"The button is here somewhere I just need to find it, it's **att**ach**e**d to a small track and keeps moving so if someone, an **in**tru**de**r breaks in they can't go any further."

After a few more minutes he was still looking and I started to feel **nerv**ous, I wasn't sure where he was taking me, or **wheth**er he really was crazy. Was this a trap I **th**ough**t,** did he bring me in here for Sam and Darren?

It was at that point a section in the floor slid open. I looked down and saw stairs leading down underground.

"Come on", Peter said **encouragingly** and started to walk down the stairs.

I followed, **wondering whether** I was doing the right thing or not, I would soon find out.

We must of walked down two hundred steps before we **reach**ed a **huge** room, it was so big, the same size as a football pitch. Inside there was a large **comput**er screen with **switch**es and **dial**s on a keyboard. It also had in it a sofa, TV, fridge and even an Air Hockey table.

"Wow Peter, this is **awe**some, how did you do all of this without anyone **k**nowing?" I asked in **amaze**ment.

Peter **replie**d, " Well I had a little help, I wasn't **entirely** or **tot**ally honest with you. It is not just me who can use this room; there is a group of us who are here on Earth for a **special** reason. I think you know what I am talking about Jonny."

Feeling scared, thinking this might be a trap I asked Peter to **explain** what he meant, he **continue**d to talk:

"I knew when you walked into the classroom that you were the one we had been waiting for. There is an **evil** leader from the planet Pluto who wants to take over the **univer**se starting with Earth; every other planet has sent a **representative** to stand and fight together to stop him. We have been watching for years now, but then Darren and Sam arrived last week and we knew the time was nearly here. We just needed someone from Mars, with your **special** powers, you are the only one who can beat him Jonny."

I was stunned, "What special powers?" I asked, "I can only communicate with animals and hear from a distance. I can't beat the head leader of Planet Pluto, and who are these other people you are talking about, where are they now?"

At that moment the door flew open. I couldn't believe my eyes. Tom, Amy, Beth and Sarah ran into the room.

"What's happening Peter?" Tom yelled.

"Why is Jonny here?" Sarah interrupted, "I thought we agreed I would speak to him tonight".

Everyone started to talk at once, ignoring me completely. I felt as if I was not there and the noise was getting too much.

"Quiet!" I shouted, everyone stopped and looked at me. I started to explain what had happened this morning.

Chapter 7

Special Powers

When everyone had calmed down we all sat around a large table, and Sarah brought us a drink and a biscuit.

Tom spoke first, "We are all here for a reason Jonny, the elders of the universe have chosen each one of us for our special powers. They have brought us together to defeat the Leader of Pluto and his followers, the Plutarians.

I am from Uranus; I am able to control the weather. Amy is from Saturn, she can communicate with nature. Peter is here from Earth, he has the ability to understand technology, it is as if he can speak to the computers. Sarah is also from Earth she doesn't have any powers but she looks after us and makes sure we stay healthy.

Beth is from Venus; whatever she draws can come to life. We thought Beth was the one, who could save us, but then you arrived and we knew you were the one. That's why she has been a bit distant with you I suppose"

I looked over at Beth, she looked embarrassed, "Sorry" she whispered and gave me a small smile.

I waited a minute to take it all in and then I replied, " But I don't know what my special powers are, apart from communicating with animals and that won't save the Earth."

Sarah got up and walked over to sit beside me. She took my hand and said. "Jonny, you have a very special gift, you can do anything, just as long as you believe in yourself."

"I don't understand," I said.

Tom **explained,** " Jonny if you really **belie**ve you can do something, anything, then you will be able to do it. I can tell this is a shock to you and you have not used this power before.

We must **pract**ise we don't have long. Didn't you say they are planning the attack at the weekend? That only gives us four more days.

Peter can you close down all the **e**l**ectri**city in the school so they have to send us home? We can meet back here in one hour and get started."

On that note my new family got up from the table and left, leaving me alone with Peter. Peter was working on the **comput**er shutting down the **electri**city. He did this so the lights, **comput**ers and heating wouldn't work. A few moments later he said:

"We should go Jonny, the bell will ring soon for the end of lunch, and we don't want you getting into **trou**b**le** on your first day".

We walked back into the classroom and the first people I could see were Sam and Darren. They both looked at me and started to **laugh**, "Where have you been Jonny boy?" Sam asked, "We have been looking for you, we **th**ough**t** you might want to play football."

I just walked past not looking at them and sat at my desk. I sat and waited for the teacher to tell us to go home so I could get as far away from them, and start planning what I was going to do to save planet Earth.

Eventually the teacher told us that we could go home. There was a cheer from the class and I **sigh**e**d** with **relie**f. All I had to worry about now was Sam and Darren. I didn't want them to follow us to our **secre**t hideout. I looked **ner**vously over to Peter, it was if he could read my mind as he **w**h**ispere**d, "Don't worry about it, I have it covered."

Just when the class had packed up and everyone was about to leave, the teacher spoke again; "I have one more message, can Sam and Darren please go and see the headmaster, he would like your help moving some tables in the big hall".

They both turned around and **glared** at me, but I just looked away. As soon as they left the room, we got up and ran back to the hide out.

We arrived to find the others waiting for us. "Right then", Tom said, "lets get started".

He sat me down in a chair in front of him while the others watched. "Jonny I want you to try and **belie**ve you can fly".

I looked at him as if he was telling a joke. 'That's **ridicul**ous, of course I can't fly, your just being really silly."

Tom **sighe**d, "OK lets start small, let's see if you can move the glass on the table. You really need to **concentrate** Jonny, you need to **belie**ve you can do it."

I looked at the glass, could I really get this to move? In my head I started to talk to the glass, I felt stupid, but I knew I had to give it a go.

"*Move glass, come on glass, come over here to me.*" **Noth**ing **happen**ed. I looked at the others; they were all **st**aring at me with hope in their eyes.

I looked back at the glass, "*I can do this,*" I told myself, "*I can move that glass.*" Still **noth**ing **happen**ed then I closed my eyes and **imag**ined that I picked the glass up with my hand and moved it across the table.

All of a **sudd**en I heard a **gasp**, as I opened my eyes, the glass smashed.

"You did it Jonny," Amy **cheer**ed as she came over to me and gave me a big hug.

"Well done mate," Peter said, slapping me hard on the back.

Sarah smiled and kissed the top of my head, and Beth just nodded in approval.

"That was great Jonny, now we just need to keep **practising** and stay **focused**," Tom said **seriously**. He had changed, he wasn't the young, relaxed, sports playing dude I first met.

Chapter 8

Preparations

By Thursday I was **exhausted**, Tom had me **practising** moving everything from the **knife** and fork at dinnertime, scoring goals whilst sitting on the side lines, changing channels on the TV and **switch**ing the lights off at night.

School wasn't much better. I had Sam and Darren following me around everywhere, **whispering** to each other. Even **th**ough I could hear them talking, I couldn't understand what they where saying anymore, it was as if they were speaking a **different lang**uage.

Friday came and the big game was tomorrow, that was our deadline. I still didn't feel ready; I couldn't understand how I could save planet Earth. I still couldn't make myself **belie**ve that I could fly. I felt so **nerv**ous and **scared**; maybe tomorrow was going to be my last living day.

It was Friday evening and Peter came to our house for tea. Sarah cooked my **favourite** Fish Fingers, Cheese Potato and Baked Beans. It looked so **tast**y, but I wasn't **hungry**. I looked around the table and no one was talking, everyone was wrapped up in their own **th**oughts, thinking about tomorrow.

I asked to leave the table and said I was going for a walk. Tom and Peter got up to follow me, but I asked them to stay, I really needed some time to myself. They were not happy but they understood and let me go.

I walked out of the house, everything was still and so **quiet**, there was no wind and the moon was full and bright. I started walking not really **knowing** where I was going; I was just putting one foot in front of the other.

After I while I found myself at school, I was going to head to the hideout and then I saw the woods, and I **thought** about Devin. I **wondered** if he was in there somewhere so I started heading towards the trees.

It was dark in the woods but it felt safe somehow, I knew there were wolves in there, but I was no longer afraid of them. I walked **deeper** into the woods looking and calling out Devin's name but **nothing happened**, he didn't **appear**.

I started to grow **tired** and wanted to find somewhere to sit when I spotted something familiar a bunch of leaves and **branches piled** up. My ship! What with everything that went on I had almost **forgotten** about my ship. It was **invisible** so I couldn't see it; I **reached** out my hands and felt around until I felt the **switch**. I pressed it and slowly it came **visible** again. I could see the **damage** from the crash, I wondered if I would ever be able to fix it?

I opened it up and climbed in, it felt so good to be in there, I started to think about home and my family. I missed them so much, I just wanted to hug my mum, and play wrestling with my brother and sister. I wished I could talk to my Dad right now, as he always knew what to do. I couldn't **though**, he wasn't here, none of them were, and I wasn't sure if I would ever see them again. How could I win this battle tomorrow when I wasn't ready to fight?

I was looking inside to see if there was anything I could use for tomorrow, if I had any sap left. (I might need to use it if they **attack** me and I hurt myself.) Then I heard a sound, I sat still, listening. It sounded like something **whispering** my name. I looked out of the window in my ship and saw Devin standing there looking in.

"Devin!" I shouted, as I jumped out of the ship. I was so pleased to see him. He nodded his head and looked deep into my eyes.

"Hello Jonny, how are you?" He asked, "I have been waiting to see you, I **wondered** when you would come back to find your ship".

We sat down and talked, I told him everything that had **happen**e**d** to me, and about the battle that was going to **h**appen tomorrow. I told him about my **spec**ial powers, but I didn't think I could use because I didn't really **bel**i**e**ve I could win the battle. Devin listened carefully not saying a word.

Finally he spoke, "Jonny you will be fine, you have to win this not only to save the Earth but for your own family. They sent you here because they **believe**d in you. They know you can do this.

I will be here in the woods waiting Jonny; if you need any help out there tomorrow all you need to do is ask.

You need to go home and rest now, you have big day tomorrow, and Sarah and your friends will be **worrie**d about you. Here jump on my back and I will give you a ride."

I got on Devin's back; he asked me if I was ready, when I nodded he set off. Slowly at first, but once he felt I was **secur**e he ran like the wind. He ran so fast, he made my eyes water, and I had to hold on tight to his antlers.

When we got to the house, I jumped off Devin and thanked him. "**Rem**em**ber** what I said Jonny," he said and then he turned around, and he was gone.

I walked into the house and everyone was in the hallway waiting for me. I told them I was OK and that I just needed to go to bed. I **quie**t**ly** walked up the stairs and into my room. I didn't know how I was going to rest, but once my head hit the pillow my eyes started to shut and I fell into a deep sleep.

Chapter 9

The Big Day

I woke suddenly, I had slept, but it had been restless. I had dreamt that I was playing in a football game, and I was losing, I was in goal and opposition were shooting ball after ball burying me in the netting.

It was early when I got up and the sun was just rising. I looked into Tom's bed but he was not there, so I went downstairs to find everyone already sitting around the breakfast table.

"You need to eat something Jonny, you will need the energy for later," Sarah told me as she pulled out a chair and gestured me to sit down. I knew she was right, so I poured myself a bowl of cereal and slowly tried to force it down.

"We need to go over our plan," Tom said seriously,

"The battle is going to take place during the football match, I know that for sure. Peter has changed the school team list so myself, Amy, Beth and Jonny are on the team. It is one of the schools rules to include all students so we should get away with it.

 It will be our job to make sure the other team players do not get hurt, and we need to get them off the pitch as soon as the battle begins. Peter you can organise an announcement over the speaker?"

Peter nodded.

"Peter what do we need to know about the planet Pluto and Plutarians that live there?" Amy asked.

Peter **answered,** " I have **search**ed everywhere and I couldn't find much out. I know that Pluto is a tiny planet made up of rock and ice, it is the last planet in the **univers**e before the **Kui**per belt, which is a huge ring of frozen rocks. So they must be able to work with a cold **clim**ate.

Pluto is the only planet that's **orbit**s the sun on a **different** path, the rest of our planets go around the sun at nearly the same level. If the **Plutarians** take over the Earth they will have an insight to the other planets within the **univers**e.

That is all I could find, I don't know what powers they have."

"Thank you Peter," Tom **re**plied, "we must set off for school, has everyone got what they need for the game? If not go now, we will be leaving in ten minutes."

We got up from the table and went off to get ready for school. I felt sick, all I could think that this may be the last day of my life".

We all got into the car and Sarah drove to us to school, the car was silent, we didn't talk, and I just looked out of the window. It was **spook**y as everything was the same as always. People were saying goodbye to each other, rushing to school or work. Some were walking their dogs or **coll**ecting their post. These people had no idea that in just a few hours, it could be the end of the world. I felt sorry for them.

Peter and I walked into the classroom, the first thing I did was look for Sam and Darren, but they weren't there, their desks were **em**pty. I asked the teacher where they were. She told me that they had gone to welcome the visitors who were here for the football game, which was to be played later that afternoon. It was their job to make them **com**for**ta**ble and to show them where everything is.

I looked at Peter; I didn't need to say anything. We both understood each other's feelings.

I never knew time to go so slow; I **thought** the morning would never end. I didn't do any work, just **sketch**ed a plan of the football pitch and the best **positi**on to be in.

Finally the bell went, the teacher **announce**d that after lunch we should all meet in the school gym, as there was going to be a school football match in the afternoon. Those who were taking part should go **straigh**t to the changing rooms.

Even **though** I **tri**ed I couldn't eat the sandwiches Sarah had packed for me, they felt like pieces of sandpaper in my mouth. I looked around the table and everyone was the same, apart from Peter who was eating everything in sight, as if it was the last meal he was ever going to have.

We waited for Peter to finish, then Tom, Amy, Beth and myself, said goodbye and headed off to the changing rooms. After wishing each other good luck the girls went one way, and we went into the boys changing rooms.

We met again in the large gym where the team captain **greet**ed us and **introduc**ed us to the rest of the team, (who didn't look very happy we were playing). We were told what **positi**ons we were to play. Tom was in **attack**, both Amy and Beth in midfield and I was playing in defence.

After a pre match talk the captain nodded and **gestur**ed that we head onto the pitch. I walked out of the door and I couldn't **belie**ve my eyes.

All eleven boys of the other team looked **ex**actly like Sam and Darren, all had dark, spiky hair and blue eyes with a hint of **purple**. All of them **smirk**ing at us, a smile so evil I will never forget it. I soon worked out that there were eleven of them against four of us, if you **include**d Peter and his **comput**er that made five. I wasn't sure how Peter's **comput**er could help in the battle, and at that moment in time I wasn't even sure how I could help **either**.

We took our places, I looked around to see Sarah on the sidelines, she smiled, and then the **whistle** blew and the game began.

Chapter 10

The Game

At first it seemed like an **ord**inary game of football, we even scored a couple of goals, I started to think that maybe I was wrong and it was just a game of football, not a battle that my life **depend**ed on. That's when things started to **h**appen.

First I **noticed** the ball was getting cold and it felt harder every time I kicked it. It was when one of our teammates headed the ball and let out a loud **scream**. I looked round and **s**aw him lying on the floor **uncon**scious, he looked dead with blood **pouring** from his head. The **Plutarian** team had turned the ball to ice.

They **laugh**ed and started to kick the ball harder, trying to hit the other players who were running around the pitch. The ball did hit another boy, and he fell down holding his leg crying and shouting. His leg was **brok**en.

That was it the battle had begun and we needed to get the **in**nocent students and **by**standers away from the pitch, and into the school gym where they would be safe.

I gave the signal to Sarah and she ran to the hideout. I could see Amy she standing in the middle of the pitch looking up to the sky with her arms raised up, shouting "wind", over and over again. The louder the **chanting** got, the stronger the wind became, then all of a **sudd**en a huge **g**ust of leaves blew onto the pitch. No one could see a thing, and the leaves **stu**ng our eyes. A loud beep came over a large **sp**eaker, then Sarah's voice came out telling everyone that there is a **sev**ere weather warning and they should all make there way to the school gym. The match was now **cancell**ed.

I **noticed** people leaving in a hurry. Then there was just the four of us and eleven of them. How the hell were we going to win this?

Amy couldn't carry on for much longer, **creating** such a storm and holding it for so long **drained** all the **energy** out of her. The wind started to die down and the pitch was clear again. I **noticed** Amy **slumped** in the middle of the pitch, I shouted to Beth who ran and dragged Amy to **shelter** at the side.

The **Plutarians** eyes were now **completely purple**, with Beth **nursing** Amy, Peter and Sarah in the hideout that left myself and Tom. The other team started to walk towards us **laughing**. I stepped back and bumped into Tom, we were **surrounded**. I called for to the animals asking if any of them could help me.

There was a **screeching noise,** and all of a **sudden** birds from all **different breeds** flew out of the trees and started **swooping** down, **pecking** at the heads of the boys. They **crouched** down for cover, but the birds kept on coming **pecking** and **pecking**. Tom and I **managed** to get away from the middle of the **circle** and stood to watch the birds at work. Then we **noticed** one **Plutarian** player fall to the ground along with **another** and **another** within **seconds** about five players had **disappeared**. It was the rabbits digging holes big **enough** for the players to fall **through**.

I started to **laugh,** looking at Tom I said, "That's it Tom, at this rate we will have won the game, and will be home in time for some supper!"

"I don't think so Jonny," Tom said his face had turned white. He was pointing behind me, I looked back and I could see at least **another twenty Plutarian** boys walking towards the pitch, **touching** the **swooping** birds and turning them to ice.

I turned back round in **horror** to talk to Tom, but he had his eyes closed tight. I could see he was **concentrating, muttering** words **quietly** under his breath.

The sky grew darker and darker as rain clouds came in to **hover** over the pitch. Then it started to rain, the rain came down so hard and fast it hurt when it hit. The pitch soon got muddy and boys where **slid**ing about everywhere, falling into holes, but still more boys kept coming.

Amy ran back onto the pitch to help, pushing boys over wherever she could. She was doing well and they were going down like flies, until I spotted **anoth**er **Pluta**rian boy with his eyes shut also **concentrat**ing like Tom. All of a **sudde**n it turned really cold and the raindrops had turned to ice, now hailstones were falling on us.

All Tom could do was open his eyes to stop the rain, so the hailstones could no longer fall. The boys had **collect**ed the hailstones and started to throw them at us. Every time they hit it took a **layer** of skin off, which **stu**ng.

I could see Amy again, she was **struggling** under the **attack,** but she was strong and kept **throw**ing hailstones back, pushing the boys over as they ran passed. Amy also **managed** to **cre**ate a **torna**do that spun around the pitch **k**nocking all them over.

Tom was making it rain in short downpours wetting the boys. He **m**anaged to stop each downpour before the boy could turn them to hailstones.

Again, I felt a little hope that we were on the winning team. There **w**ere now only nine boys on the **op**posing team.

That is when I saw Sam and Darren; they began to grow taller than the other boys. Amy ran to push Darren over but as she got close, he **reach**ed out and **touch**ed the top of her head – she turned to Ice. I **scream**ed at Tom, because he was **nea**rer to Amy and he ran over to help her. It only took one sharp turn from Darren and Tom was frozen too.

Now there was just me **against** nine boys, **includ**ing Sam and Darren who were now as tall as a two-storey **house**.

I could see Sam holding a stick, he was walking towards the school, his eyes **shinn**ing bright **purple.** I knew he was on his way to brainwash the students. I turned to run at him, but as I looked around I could see the **re**m**aining** eight boys **clos**ing in and **surround**ing me, giving me that same evil smile and **laugh**ing.

I needed help and fast.

Chapter 11

The End

The boys were getting **closer** and **closer**, I was **desperate** and in need of help, so I shouted for the only living animal I knew who could help me – Devin. Within **seconds** he was standing by my side along with **another** ten deer behind him. "We have been waiting for you. I didn't think you were going to call," he said.

I smiled and they began to charge at the other boys while I started to make my way to Sam. We didn't get very far, just as Devin and his herd were **approaching** the boys, Darren **touch**ed the football pitch and it turned to ice. We all slid, and I fell on my arm, the pain shot **through** my body like I had been hit by **lightning**. I looked and Sam was nearly at the doors of the school, a few **minutes** more and he will be inside.

I felt like crying, I was losing the battle, when I heard Beth shout, – "Jonny, get ready!" She had a **sketch**book and pencil, was drawing **frantically**, as if she was really **excited**. I forgot Beth was with us; she had been hiding behind the bins waiting for her moment to come.

Suddenly my football boots started to change, I was now **wearing** ice skates and so were Devin and his herd. I had never seen anything as **strange** as deer ice-skating. I hadn't been on an ice rink before; I **carefully** got up and slowly put one foot in front of the other. I could skate and I was fast, I headed towards the school.

I wasn't fast **enough though**, I saw Sam **reach** the school doors and **crawl** in. I **th**ought that was it, the end. I looked around and saw the frozen **statue**s of Amy and Tom, the deer were trying to catch the boys but now they had the advantage and Darren was turning them to ice one by one. Peter and Sarah were in the hideout trying to find out anything they could to beat the Plutarians, and stop all communications with the emergency services. (There was nothing they could do, and the last thing I needed was trying to explain this situation to the police).

My friends were hurt and I felt a rush of anger my body grew hotter and hotter, I could hear the blood pumping in my head. I knew then only I could save the Earth, I knew what I had to do.

I called to Beth and shouted, "wings!" She nodded and started to draw, but as I shouted Darren saw her too and started running in her direction. I could feel a tickling sensation on my back. I turned towards Beth and I saw Darren touch her head. The feeling stop and my heart sank.

"Just believe Jonny, you just need to believe!" Devin shouted as he skated past me ducking out of the way of Darren's touch. I closed my eyes and told myself *I can fly. I have to I have to save the others. I can fly.* I started to skate as fast as I could and I felt my feet lift off the ground. I opened my eyes and I was in the air, I was really flying.

As I flew passed the hideout I looked down and I saw Sarah holding a large sheet of paper. It read:

"THE EYES!"

That was it! I could beat them by the eyes. I headed straight for the school, when I reached the doors I lowered myself down and walked inside making my way to the sports hall. When I got there Sam had shrunk to the same size as an average adult, he was taking one child at a time and putting his stick to their heart. The stick turned bright yellow and then the child did, after that they fell into a deep sleep.

I took a deep **breath**; **straighten** my back and walked towards him.

"I don't think so Sam, you can't win this one," I said as **confidently** as I could.

At first Sam looked **stunned**, and then he smiled and **replied**, " You really think you can beat me little Jonny, with what? Your friends are frozen, and you have **nothing**."

"I **believe**," I said **quickly**.

Sam **laughed**, "In what? What have you got to **believe** in?"

At that, he turned around to pick **another** child, I felt the anger rush **through** my body again, and I began to feel the heat burn inside me. Then **suddenly** I knew the **answer**, heat. The heat could hurt Sam as his powers were ice, the heat could melt his powers.

Slowly I said, " I **believe** in myself Sam", he turned around to look at me again, but this time I could see the **panic** in his eyes. For the first time he was scared.

My whole body **flickered** with flames, I put my hands together and threw a fireball at his feet he jumped up, but it **skimmed** his toes and they started to steam. The fire went out.

Sam started to run towards me **throwing** ice, when it **touched** me the fire would go out. I had to **concentrate** hard and stay **focused** to keep my fire going. *'I can win this,'* I **thought**.

I climbed up the ladder and along the top of the wooden beams in the roof. Sam followed, **although** he stayed on the floor and **blasted** shots of ice **through** his stick. I **dodged, throwing** fireballs back at him. It seemed to go on for hours, and I started to get **tired**.

At that point Sam shouted, "You can't stay up there all day Jonny!" That is when he sent a shot of ice to the beam. The beam **cracked** in two and I fell to the floor.

I lay on my back looking up, I could see black dots in my eyes and I could here Sam's footsteps walking towards me.

"You were wrong Jonny. I can do this! You should **believe** in the **Plutarians** you are **noth**ing," he said.

I started to **believe** him; I was stupid to think that I could ever beat him and the **Plutarians**. I closed my eyes to **prepare** myself for the **att**ack and waited. When I heard my dad's **voice** in my head, he was saying, *"Don't give up Jonny, you must never give up".*

I felt that rush of anger rise in me again, I wasn't going to let this bully win. I opened my eyes a little and **wh**ispered back "I can't hear you Sam. Help me please?"

He came close to my face, and started to speak.

It was then I **believed** in my last fireball and threw it into his eyes.

Chapter 12

Help

I didn't have time to think I needed to help Devin; he was still out there with the other **Plutarian** boys. I got up, took Sam's stick and ran out of the school, but it was all **quiet**. Devin, Peter and Sarah stood still in shock.

"Where are they all?" I asked.

"I don't know what you did in there Jonny, but a bright **purple** light shone from the school. When it did the boys stopped and ran off into the woods **screaming**."

I started to **explain** what had **happened,** but I **noticed** the football pitch and everyone was still frozen, and inside the school there were **thirty** boys and girls in a deep sleep brainwashed. We needed to help them.

I turned to Devin and asked, "The students need the sap from the plants. Can you go to my ship and find some?" Before I could finish **speaking** he ran off into the woods.

I walked over to the one of the deer and placed my hand on his head. "*I believe I can help, I can make you better*". I **imagined** heat from my hand **warming** the deer, my hand **glowed** red and the deer started to melt.

I went to Tom, Amy and Beth and did the same. Sarah had **gathered** some **towels** from the hide out which she wrapped around each one of them.

Slowly one by one the deer, birds and rabbits came back to life and **huddled** together. Devin soon came back with some sap so Peter and I went into the school to help the children. We placed a spoonful in each of their mouths and gave everyone else a hot drink with the sap juice inside it.

People started to come around; they looked **dazed** (as if they could not work out what had **happened)**.

The parents and teachers started to talk fast, asking each other questions, but no one knew the answers.

Peter looked at me for an **explanation**, I told him "the sap from the plants, heals **injuries** but it also helps people forget."

We both **sneaked** out before anyone could spot us. I saw Devin and he looked at me, **lowered** his head and took his herd off into the woods. The birds flew off and the rabbits **disappeared** underground.

I stood with Peter, Tom, Amy, Beth and Sarah looking at the football pitch and the mess it was in. I didn't know how it was going to be **explained**.

"Maybe they will just think it was a bad storm," Beth said, "Amy did start the **violent** winds at the **beginning** of the battle."

Then I heard in the **distance** the police **sirens**, I knew they were coming this way. "I think we should head home, the police are coming," I suggested.

Everyone agreed and we walked towards Sarah's car.

Chapter 13

Holidays

All the local newspapers had front cover stories about the strange storm that destroyed Whitehall School's football pitch. The papers commented on how strange it was that nobody could remember the storm or what had happened inside the gym. Police were investigating.

The school was closed the following week due to police looking around to see if they could find any clues. We decided to stay away from the school until all of the attention died down. This suited me fine, I was so tired and slept for a whole two days, only waking to eat and drink.

I dreamt of my family, but I wasn't sad anymore, in the battle I heard my Dad speak to me, I knew he would be proud, and I knew they were safe. I was sure that one day I would be able to go home. I thought that when I am allowed to go back into school I would go into the woods and thank Devin, his herd and the other animals. I would also see if I could start to repair my ship.

Tom seemed more relaxed and played the sports games on the X box with Peter. (Unlike in real life Peter won every game and was enjoying the victory).

Amy and Beth helped Sarah bake cakes and repaint their bedroom upstairs; it was back to normal and no one mentioned what happened last Friday.

We all had the same thought, what happened to the Plutarians, did they really just disappear or will they be back for revenge? Days went by and nothing unusual had happened, but in the house tension started to grow, as none of us knew what was going to happen next, and no one wanted to talk about it.

It was one night when we sat around the kitchen table eating our supper, when Sarah announced she had enough of the uneasy feeling between us all, and she had booked a holiday so we could go and relax.

I was happy, it would be nice to see more of planet Earth, and for once I could act my age.

We were going somewhere warm to enjoy the sun, sea, sand and most importantly each other's company.

It was a good feeling knowing that I would not have to think about fighting the Plutarians for a while, or would I?

Printed in Great
Britain
by Amazon